It Takes Balance

Diane Bair and Pamela Wright

Contents

Rigby

It Takes Balance

Close your eyes and try to stand on one foot. Did you sway or lose your balance? Have you ever tried to walk across a log? Did you lose your balance then? Sometimes keeping your balance is difficult to do!

Some athletes need amazing balancing skills to perform their sports.

- Jumping up, flipping in midair, and landing on a 4-inch beam . . .

Did You Know?

How does your body balance? It uses signals from your eyes, legs and trunk, and inner ears.

How do you
think athletes develop
balancing skills?

- Standing on a surfboard as it rides a raging, tumbling wall of water . . .
- Balancing on a snowboard as it races down a steep, slippery mountain.

Gymnastics, surfing, snowboarding . . . these sports take super balance!

3

Flips, Rolls, and Tumbles

Have you ever watched a **gymnast** leap, twirl, and flip in the air? Gymnasts perform amazing **feats** of strength and balance.

Sometimes, gymnasts must balance on their hands. On the pommel horse, a gymnast does handstands and swings by holding on to the handles.

The gymnast may not touch any other part of the horse.

The gymnast balances on one hand and swings his legs.

Gymnastic Events

Balance beam

Floor exercise

Rings

Pommel horse

Uneven bars

Parallel bars

Do you think
some people are
"natural gymnasts"?
Why do you
think so?

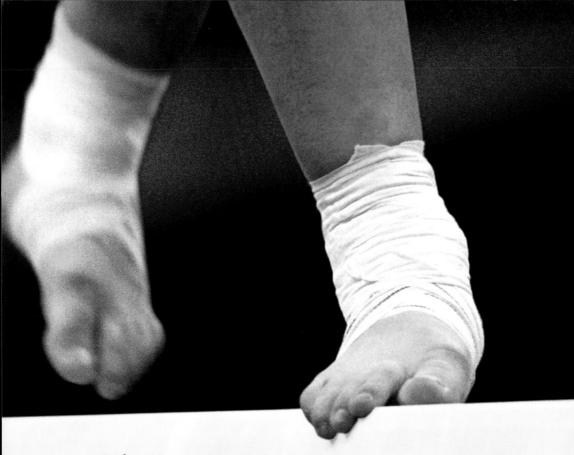

What is a piece of wood almost 4 feet off the floor but only 4 inches wide? It's a balance beam! Top gymnasts perform somersaults, jumps, and handsprings on it. **Routines** on the balance beam last between 75 and 90 seconds, and the entire time gymnasts must try not to wobble, stop, or fall. No wonder it's called the *balance* beam!

How do you think gymnasts might feel before a routine? Why do you think they might feel this way?

Emily, a young gymnast, says, "At first, I couldn't even walk across the balance beam without falling off. But now I'm doing leaps and jumps. It just takes practice."

Thousands of kids across the country are taking gymnastics classes. Would you?

Catching the Big Wave

Picture yourself riding on top of a giant ocean wave as it tumbles and roars to the shore. What a thrill! But learning to stand up on a surfboard is not easy. It takes practice and balance!

To stand up, surfers must jump to their feet in one quick movement. Their feet should land in the center of the board, one foot slightly in front of the other. Then they must lean forward or backward to make the surfboard **skim** evenly along the water. Surfers bend their knees and hold their arms out for balance.

Do you think you would like to learn how to surf? Why or why not?

A surfer must know the correct foot placement
in order to stand on a board.

If surfers lean too far forward, the nose of their boards will dive into the water. If they lean too far backward, the board will shoot out from under them. Finding the right balance is important.

Bruce Gabrielson is a former surfing champion and founder of the first high-school surfing league in the United States. He says, "Usually by the second or third time out, beginners start to have some balance and are able to catch a wave. From this point on, the more you surf, the better you get!"

Now that you've learned a little more about surfing, have you changed your opinion about whether you'd like to try it? Why or why not?

Surfing is a lot like skateboarding. Turning a surfboard is similar to turning a skateboard with smooth moves on a hill.

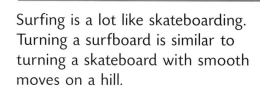

HIGH SURF

Bumps, Banks, and Big Air

Could you stand on one foot and balance for a count of 20? If you can, you're ready to try snowboarding!

Mikey Franco is a snowboard teacher in Wyoming. "Balance is **essential** for this sport," he says. Franco teaches his students how to balance on the snowboard with their knees bent and their arms out.

Do you think you would like to snowboard? Why or why not?

Did You Know?

Compared with gymnastics and surfing, snowboarding is a young sport. It started in the mid-1960s. Snowboarding is now an Olympic sport.

Snowboarders can't be afraid to take a tumble through the air into a snowbank. "When you're learning to snowboard, you fall a lot!" says Franco. "Everybody does." Snowboarders must learn how to turn and stop by shifting their weight over the board.

With a little practice, snowboarders can soon ride down the mountain. Before long, many of them are zipping through a half-pipe—a long tubelike area with high snowbanks. They're sailing over bumps and catching "big air"!

How do you think snowboarders feel catching "big air"?

All snowboarders turn by shifting their weight.

Did You Know?

Snowboarding started
when Tom Sims designed
the "ski board" as part
of an 8th grade
wood shop project.

Wrap It Up

Good balance is important in many sports. Why do gymnastics, surfing, and snowboarding require good balancing skills?

turning

stopping

standing

Snowboarding

Which of these sports do you think would be the hardest to do? Why do you think that?

Good Balance

Gymnastics

Surfing

pommel horse

balance beam

standing up

standing up on board